❖ A Ballad of the ❖
CIVIL WAR

✦ A Ballad of the ✦

CIVIL WAR

by **MARY STOLZ**

illustrated by
SERGIO MARTINEZ

SCHOLASTIC INC.
New York Toronto London Auckland Sydney

To Joel Barr, in friendship

ISBN 0-590-81926-7

Copyright © 1997 by Mary Stolz.
Illustrations copyright © 1997 by HarperCollins Publishers, Inc.
All rights reserved. Published by Scholastic Inc., 555 Broadway, New York, NY 10012, by arrangement with HarperCollins Children's Books, a division of HarperCollins Publishers.

12 11 10 9 8 7 6 5 4 3   8 9/9 0 1 2 3/0

Printed in the U.S.A.   40
First Scholastic printing, October 1998

CONTENTS

ON AN EVENING IN AUGUST 1862, Tom Rigby, lieutenant in the Sixth Union Cavalry, returning from reconnaissance, rode through a storm toward camp.

Soldiers of both armies—Union and Confederate—struggled through mud, blood, and wind-tossed rain. The sound of distant cannon fire vied with thunder, and the dead lay in ditches, next to a rutted road lit now and then by flashes of lightning.

Almost asleep in the saddle, Tom jerked upright as his horse, Pompety, stumbled.

"Tired, are you?" he said, leaning to pat the drooping neck. "And hungry, too, I know. So am I hungry, and tired, and I haven't washed for days."

Damp and drowsing, horse and rider splashed on.

Again Lieutenant Rigby leaned over and spoke in his horse's ear.

"Pompety, this is the twenty-fourth of August, 1862. Today I am twenty-one years old, and a long, long way from home."

The horse, accustomed to his rider's conversation, made a motion with his head.

"I am thinking, Pompety," the young officer went on, wiping rain from his face. "I am thinking of Jack. My twin. We shared nineteen years, nineteen birthdays. Now I don't even know where he is, or how he is, or if he is even still alive. And he knows no more of me."

He'd been keeping his eyes down, to avoid the nightmare around him, but now a figure at the roadside seized his attention. A soldier in a bloodied rebel uniform sat, arms around his knees, quietly crying.

Dismounting, Lieutenant Rigby approached the huddled figure.

"Jack?" he whispered. "Is it you, Jack?"

CHAPTER ONE

O N THE MORNING OF AUGUST 24, 1850, Tom Rigby woke early, then lay considering the day ahead. There was going to be a party on this, the ninth birthday of the Rigby twins.

That's us, Tom thought comfortably. Jack and me. We're nine years old.

It was to a big, *big* party. Their mother had been planning it for ages.

Friends and relations, neighbors from nearby plantations, would be arriving with their children, and with lots and lots of gifts. There would be, in Tom's opinion, too many gifts and too many grown-ups waiting to be thanked too much.

Still, he thought, a party is a party and maybe it'll be fun.

He yawned, smiled, looked over at Jack, sound asleep, gently snoring.

"Jack!" he yelled. "Wake up, wake up! We're nine years old today!"

"Call me when we're twenty," mumbled Jack, pulling a pillow over his head.

Tom laughed, got washed and dressed, and bounded downstairs to the kitchen, where Roger, the butler, was polishing silver and Tulitha, the cook, was kneading spongy bread dough.

"Morning, Uncle Roger," said Tom. "Morning, Tulitha! That smells wonderful!"

The cook continued her work in silence, but the butler smiled. "Morning to you, young Tom. Up betimes, as usual, I see."

"Jack's asleep. He won't be nine years old for the first time in his life ever again. But he says we're to call him when we're twenty."

"Can't wait to be all grown up and his own man, our Jack."

Tom shrugged. "Far's I'm concerned, I'm my own man now. Where's Aaron?"

"Down to the quarter."

"When'll he be back?"

"Won't be back."

Tom scowled. "Uncle *Roger*, quit funning. I don't like that."

"Not funnin', Tom. Aaron's been sent to the quarter. For good and all."

"What are you talking about? This's the birthday party day. Why's Aaron down there 'stead of up here?"

"Tom, don't devil me. The plain fact, no way 'round it, is that Aaron's stayin' in the quarter from now on."

Tom stamped his foot. "That's crazy!"

"Call it anyway you wants, it's a settled matter."

"No, it ain't! Isn't! I'm going right down there and fetch him back home."

"No, Tom! That's jes' what you won't do. You gonna leave well enough alone."

"Why? It isn't *well enough* at all. It's *awful.* So why should I leave it alone?"

"Because. That's why," said Roger, polishing a heavy ladle harder, as if trying to erase its intricate design.

Tulitha plumped the mound of dough in a

large bowl, covered it with a damp linen cloth, snorted a half laugh, and walked out to the back porch, letting the door slam behind her.

Tom jerked the butler's arm. "Because? What kind of answer is *because*?"

Roger drew a deep breath, put the ladle aside. At length he met Tom's eyes. "The *because* is—because your daddy say it's time that Aaron go back where he belong."

"He belongs here. He belongs with Jack and me. You know that. He's—" Tom hesitated, then said, "He's *ours*."

Aaron, five years older than the twins, had been given to them as a christening present by Colonel Galpin, their mother's brother. Raised along with them by Aunty Bess, Aaron lived with her off the kitchen but spent most of his days with Jack and Tom, protecting and guiding them like an older brother, sharing their lives in all ways.

In almost all ways.

"A right bright darky," Mr. Rigby frequently said. "Watches out for the boys better'n any dog would."

"What's Aaron gone and done, Uncle Roger?" Tom asked. "Why's he belong down there all of a sudden like that?"

"Your daddy say he's got uppity."

"Uppity?" Tom said. *Uppity* was a bad thing to be said of any slave. "How's he got uppity? He's just the same as always."

"Your daddy say he's too free with you boys, actin' like there's no difference between you and him—"

"What's wrong with that? We haven't ever made a difference between him and us. Why should we?"

"Sometimes, Tom," Roger said impatiently, "you act like you still four years old. You *know* your daddy don't hold with white boys bein' friends with coloreds."

"That's for—for *other* people. Not Aaron."

"When your daddy say you 'n' Jack is too old now fer that kinda minglin', that's the end on it. Aaron's outgrowed his place with you."

"That's a dumb stupid crazy idea. He's practically our brother. I'm going to pull Jack out of bed right now, an' we'll go fetch him back."

"I tell you no!"

"And I say yes." Tom started off.

"You want Aaron should be sold off?"

Tom turned back. "Sold *off*! Daddy would never do that. Never!"

Roger began counting spoons.

"He wouldn't . . . would he?" Tom asked miserably.

"You go 'gainst him in this, he might conclude to put Aaron in his pocket."

That slaves were sold—putting money in their owners' pockets—and that they were bought and traded, was something Tom knew. Uncle Roger himself had come to the household long ago, in payment of gambling debts owed to their father.

But never till now had Tom thought that plantation business applied to Aaron. Aaron wasn't just anybody. Aaron was . . . he was theirs, his and Jack's.

"Uncle Roger!" he said triumphantly. "Aaron belongs to me and Jack. Daddy can't send him down to the quarter without even *asking* us. Can he?"

"Can't he?"

"Well, I'm going to see Aunty Bess, that's what I'm going to do."

"Do that."

Roger picked up a tureen and examined it closely, as if Tom had already left.

Aunty Bess, who had been nurse to the twins when they were little, put one arm around Tom. "You call to mind, Tom, the time we was in town and passed that there shambles by the railroad station, when your daddy's carriage got held up?"

"I remember," Tom said uneasily.

The shambles was a platform on which had stood a line of Negroes. Men, women, children, waiting to be sold. Tom recalled how quiet they had been. He'd been seven years old then, plenty old enough to be shocked by what he saw.

"Aunty, what's that sign say?" he'd asked.

"Don't rightly know, Tom."

A man standing nearby put his head right into the carriage.

"I'll tell you what it says, son. Says *Prime plantation hands. Healthy. Docile. Hard workers. Sold separately or in lots.* Like they were crockery, or something."

"Sir," Mr. Rigby had said, icily offended, "you just remove your face from my rig, you hear? Don't you try infectin' my young 'uns with your filthy Yankee notions."

"Your children are infected, sir. But not by me," said the man, shaking his head as he walked away.

Mr. Rigby knocked sharply on the roof of the carriage with his cane.

"Get us out of here!" he directed the coachman. "Now!"

"Why were they all so quiet, Aunty?" Tom asked now. The memory had never entirely left him.

"Scared quiet, Tom. Scared dumb."

"I don't want Aaron ever to be on a shambles."

"No, you don't want that, no way. So you best leave everythin' be. I'll tell him you miss him. Send him your regards."

"Not regards. Love. Send him my love," said Tom, moving out of her arms. "Tell him I'm—tell him we, Jack and me—say we're awful sorry he won't be at our party."

Jack, when he heard of Aaron's banishment, frowned. "Now, that's right mean. And on the day of our party, too. Shucks."

"Should we even have a party now?"

Jack looked astonished. "Tom! I'm right sorry about Aaron, but just the same . . . There's a generous lot of people and packages comin' here today, just for us two. You're tellin' me we're supposed to tell Mama that if we don't get Aaron back, we won't go to our own party? After all the plannin' she's done? Besides, what would Daddy say? What about that? He'd call it a notion."

Tom had not given his parents a thought when all his mind was taken up with Aaron. Now he hesitated.

Their father did not put up with what he called "notions" from anyone. A notion was anything he didn't approve of. Even their mother was not permitted to have them. Until today Tom had never considered having one, but it was certain sure that fighting to get Aaron back would be considered not just a notion but a monstrous defiance.

"Can you have fun without Aaron there?" he asked, and was not surprised at his brother's reply.

"I can try, Tom," said Jack. "I can sure enough try."

CHAPTER TWO

I T WAS A SOFT, SUNNY VIRGINIA AFTERNOON,
that day of their ninth birthday. Fragrant,
flowery. The Big House was shaded by lofty,
ancient trees, cooled by a tossy breeze.

From nearby plantations, neighbors on horse-
back, in carriages, in pony traps drew up to the

great portico with gifts galore, with kisses, hugs, catching-up conversations.

In the noise and bustle, the boisterous arrival of young boys and a few girls, Tom almost forgot the absence of Aaron.

"Seein' there are so many of you dear children," said Mrs. Rigby, beautiful in hoopskirt and lace, "I do believe it'd be best to open y'all's presents on the veranda, boys. Less muss and fuss."

Knowing how their parents deplored muss and fuss, the twins agreed and began eagerly to attack the mountain of offerings.

Horns, whistles, a sweet porcelain music box from an aunt who never recalled that they were boys, jack-in-the-boxes, armies of tin soldiers, wooden trains, tin drums, a parade of puppets arrayed as Crusaders, and more, much more.

"You'd think we were *six*," Jack muttered.

"This's practically the same stuff they brought us last year."

"Probably can't think of anything new," said Tom. "I *like* those hobbyhorses," he said, looking at two large, merrily painted hobbyhorses with beautiful faces and manes of real horsehair.

"Hobbyhorses! I want a horse, not a wooden toy."

"Daddy says horses when we're ten, not before. That's just a year to wait."

"A year," Jack said gloomily. "I'm tired of openin' all this stuff."

He walked over to his mother, leaned against her chair, put his arm across her shoulder. She smiled up at him.

"I declare, Mama, you smell like a flower."

"You want somethin', you scamp. Am I right?"

"Well—couldn't Uncle Roger finish up opening all this—these presents. I mean, I don't rightly believe I can open any more, and I'm right sick of sayin' thank you. 'Specially when I don't like what I'm sayin' it for."

"Now, now, Jack. Y'all wouldn't want to offend anybody—"

"I wouldn't mind, Mama. I might downright enjoy it."

"I'll see what I can do, honey," said his mother, laughing.

Tom was wishing they would all go home. He wondered how Aaron was feeling, left out of the party, banished to the quarter.

Was he, even now, looking at them from some hidden place? Staring out of the shrubbery like a cat? Concealed in a tree, in the grape arbor, somewhere no one would be looking for him?

He'll be so hurt. He won't understand.

Starting for the far end of the veranda, Tom was summoned back by his father.

"Tom! Jack!" Mr. Rigby said. "You haven't thanked Colonel Sparklehoff for that fine set of British toy soldiers." As the Colonel was quite deaf, he didn't bother to lower his voice.

"We have thousands of toy soldiers," Jack growled in Tom's ear. "I'm right sick of the sight of them."

"Mind your manners there, young man," said Mr. Rigby.

Tom sometimes felt that their father could hear even what he and Jack were thinking.

The boys moved reluctantly to where Colonel Sparklehoff, a Revolutionary War hero, sat enthroned in a wicker chair. They thanked him with proper bows, and Tom escaped before the Colonel could start telling how he had fought, in that long-ago conflict, side by side with Light-Horse Harry Lee, and General LaFayette, and even General Washington.

Jack, always fascinated by battle stories, remained for a while. When he'd had enough stories of Revolutionary generals, he edged over to where his brother was standing, asking out of the corner of his mouth, "Tom, how long are we obliged to keep on smilin'? My jaws are about to break from showin' off my teeth."

"Let's bang *hard* on those tin drums."

As they'd received about a dozen drums, there were enough for all the assembled children to make a fine racket.

A few moments of that, and Mrs. Rigby rose, suggesting that the grown-ups repair indoors to the great drawing room. As they left, she threw a smile over her shoulder at Jack, who grinned back.

★ ★ ★

"Jack!" Tom said suddenly. "Look there!"

A few slave children had ventured onto the farthest edge of the lawn. They stood gazing toward the hill of birthday presents piled helter-skelter on the large veranda.

Jack frowned. "Should they be gettin' on our lawn? I don't like that. Uppity, that's what it is."

"Don't talk that way. You sound like—"

"I sound like what?" Jack said, staring into Tom's eyes.

Like our father, thought Tom. Instead, he said, "Just sort of—mean. You don't mean to, I guess."

"Maybe I do. Do you *want* them tramplin' all over the grounds?"

Tom didn't reply. He looked toward the shabby, silent children. Aaron was not among them.

As his brother started off, Tom said, "Jack, wait! I just got an idea!"

"And I just know I'm not goin' to like it."

"Listen, will you? After the party is over, if it ever is, we'll take some of these things down there. To those children. They don't have any toys and we have too many, and we don't want most of them."

"Daddy will not like that. He won't cotton to that idea *at all*."

"We won't tell him."

"Sometimes I think you're plumb crazy," said Jack. "You've got a headful of notions, an' one of these days they'll get you into real trouble. And me along with you."

Later, when the last of the guests had departed, Mrs. Rigby instructed Uncle Roger to carry the presents up to the boys' room.

"That's a gen'rous plenty o' loot," the butler

observed to the twins. "Take a dozen trips, at the least."

"We'll leave the hobbyhorses here, where we can get at them first thing in the morning," said Tom. We can play cavalry soldiers, he thought. That should please Jack.

"Looky, Uncle Roger," Tom said. "When Mama and Daddy have gone for their siestas, I'm going to take some toys down to the children in the quarter."

"Oh, now, young Tom," Uncle Roger said. Burdened with loot, the three of them started up the broad staircase. "I don't look 'pon that to be a good idea *at all*."

"Why shouldn't they have toys, same as us?"

"If you don't know the answer to that there question, I sure 'nough am not the one to tell you."

"Anyway, I have to see Aaron, explain to him

how this is not my"—he glanced at Jack, who looked away quickly—"not *our* fault."

"Aaron won't think that 'bout you."

"I want to *tell* him."

Uncle Roger deposited an armload of packages on the floor and sighed.

"I *am* going to do it," Tom insisted. "We can give the boys all these tin soldiers. But what about the girls?"

Jack and Uncle Roger offered no suggestions.

"I know. They can have the Crusader puppets. They'll like those. I'd like to give them that music box, but there's only the one. Say—maybe Tulitha would like to have it, Uncle Roger?"

"No way would she like that. Your mother find out—*whooee!* Your daddy find out any o' this craziness, we're all in a heap o' trouble. Here an' in the quarter, too. Stirrin' up bad trouble, that's what you'll be doin'."

"Daddy never goes down to the quarter, so he won't find out unless somebody tells on us. And who'd do that?"

Uncle Roger wavered, then agreed to go along with Tom's plan, agreed that no one would tell, and hoped he was right.

Late that afternoon, Tom stole downstairs carrying a boxful of tin soldiers, all the Crusader puppets, and the fanciest of the tin drums, a red-and-gold one with silk tassels. That was for Aaron.

As he reached the veranda, Jack appeared, carrying yet more of the day's gifts.

"I knew you'd come," Tom said happily. "In the end, we're always on the same side."

"Let's get it over with," Jack said, not sounding happy at all.

CHAPTER THREE

I N A NARROW ROAD running between window-less shacks in the quarter, a flock of children appeared and stared at the twins from the Big House. They gazed in wonder at the tin soldiers, the Crusader puppets, the tasseled red-and-gold drum. They did not speak or make a move toward the toys.

Biting his lip, Tom looked to the one grown-up among them—Aaron's father, a field hand.

"Macon," Tom asked, "what's wrong? Why aren't they pleased?"

"Daresay they don't rightly understan' what y'all doin' in this here place." He looked around the quarter, then at the expensive toys, and shrugged. "Ain't never seen you here 'fore this, have we?"

Tom hunched his shoulders. "Well, can we leave—" He gestured toward what he and Jack had brought. "The—these things? For the children? For them to maybe play with after we've gone? Would that be—is that all right?"

"Reckon y'all could do that," Macon conceded.

Seeing the resentment in Jack's face, Tom said quickly, "I want to see Aaron. The drum is for him. Where is he?"

Macon lifted his shoulders, his hands.

"He can't be mad at *me*," Tom pleaded. "*I* didn't do this. I hate it for him to be down here."

"Plenty on us down here, why not Aaron? You reckon he better'n the rest of us?"

"I don't mean that. It's just that he's—" Tom couldn't finish the sentence.

"Tom, stop beggin'," Jack snapped. "Let's go! Let's go *now*!"

Tom looked at the unspeaking children, at Macon's impassive face, at the toys piled in the middle of the dirt road. Nothing had turned out the way he'd planned.

"All right," he said. "I guess you're right."

He turned again to Macon. "You know, I really thought— I guess I don't rightly know what I thought. Will you give Aaron the drum? Please."

Macon made no reply. No other grown person

appeared. The children remained silent as the brothers walked toward home.

Tom turned once and found them all standing still as statues, eyes on the ground.

A few days later, he went by himself to the quarter, hoping to find Aaron.

Down here, the late-August heat was like a hammer pounding treeless air to dust. Not a quarter of a mile off, shaded by ancient elms and oaks like enormous leafy umbrellas, the Big House seemed fragrant, almost cool.

At this time of morning, the hands were out in the tobacco, corn, and wheat fields. They'd been summoned at sunup by the overseer's horn and would work till sundown. Tom could hear them singing. They were required to do this all day long.

Tom could make out the words, but not what they meant.

Fiddle-fuddle fa da! Faddle-foddle da fa!
Up in de mawnin', up in de dawnin'
Beeses am a-swawmin', Jesus am a-comin'
Who doan know dat hornin'
Blowin' in de mawnin'
Horn horn hornin', a-blowin' in de mawnin'

A long time ago, Tom had asked Uncle Roger where the songs that sounded so lilty and felt so sad came from.

"Times they makes them up," Roger explained. "Other times sing hymns, ballads. Jes' to keep their voices up."

"But why?"

"Tom, you know the answer to that, or you ain't been payin' attention to what I tells you.

Quiet darky is a dangerous darky, accordin' to Mass' Rigby. And he's all the accordin' to gets paid any mind 'round here."

Listening to the sound of the faraway song, Tom walked aimlessly, unable to find anyone to question. It was as if the entire quarter had closed itself against him. He was turning to leave when an old woman came around a corner, a bundle of laundry balanced on her head.

They studied each other a moment before the woman spoke.

"We all glad you done give the young 'uns those there playtoys. Ain't any on them had no toys, 'fore this. Somebody should ought to say bless you, so I gives you my blessin's."

Tom smiled. "I'm glad. I mean, that they took them. I was afraid they wouldn't."

"You warn't gone a minute 'fore each chile had hisself a playtoy."

"Did Aaron get the drum? Where is he?"

She pursed her lips, started off, turned back. "Aaron won't take dat drum, nohow."

"Why?" Tom burst out.

"You bes' give up ponderin' on Aaron. He gone out to de fields 'longside of his daddy. Don't want nuthin' to do wid y'all up to the Big House any mo'. He been bad hurt, bad hurt. Don't do a bit o' good, bring a chile up in de Big House, den toss him out, used-up goods."

"But I didn't—"

"Don't matter who did what, it did got done. Young Tom, you put Aaron outta yo' mind. He done put you outta his'n, sho' sho'."

Tom walked slowly away. This time he did not look back. He wanted to be home, with his brother.

The old woman said Aaron was hurt. Bad.

Well, I'm hurt, too, Tom said to himself. Bad. And Aaron should've understood better. Should've understood *me* better.

He'd not go to the quarter again.

Daily Tom and Jack rode on their merry wooden hobbyhorses. They had named them Pompety and Brigadier. Jack now seemed quite resigned to playing at cavalry officers, men-at-arms, princes of the blood, knights of the Round Table.

They cantered across broad grassy lawns, through the keen-smelling boxwood maze, and beside a slender brownish river that rollicked its way toward a foam of steep falls downstream.

They tilted on the lawn, jousted by the river, raced each other down the mile-long elm-lined lane.

They 'played at war, at tourneys, at going on Crusade, at steeplechasing.

Now and then some children of the quarter, seeing them gallop by, waved at these boys from the Big House who had come down one day and given them toys. Something of their own to keep forever. That they could take these treasures out only after dark, and must hide them from house servants (except Roger) and the overseer, made them dearer.

No words were exchanged between them and the young masters, and Aaron was not to be seen.

Tom found that he missed Aaron less as the weeks went by.

"I won't forget him," he told Uncle Roger. "But prob'ly I can stop missing him. Like prob'ly he's stopped missing us. Missing *me*."

"That's the bes' way, young Tom. Put Aaron outta mind. Black and white cain't be frien's forever."

"Why not?" Tom shouted. "I want to know why not!"

Roger shrugged. "Y'all mus' 'scuse me now, young Tom. I got two million tasks an' only one million arms to do it all with."

One autumn day, the boys were sprinting by the river, when Jack, in the lead, stumbled and fell headlong down the bank.

Tom dropped his horse and ran to the top of the riverbank. He found Jack weeping at the water's edge, arms clasped around his knees.

"Jack!" Tom shouted, scrambling down the bank. "What is it? What's wrong?"

Rubbing his eyes, Jack pointed to what had been his horse and was now but a colored stick.

"Where's his head?" Tom demanded.

"Gone. All gone. Brigadier's nothin' but that there stick now. And I'd got to be so fond of him!" Jack said in a tearful voice.

Tom stared up and down the riverbank, but the horse's head, with its real mane and beautiful face, was not to be seen. It must have fallen into the stream and been carried away, over the falls.

Tom put a hand on his brother's shoulder. "Come on, Jack," he said. "There's room on Pompety. He'll go just as well with two."

"You tellin' me knights of the Round Table rode two to a mount?" Jack asked, sniffling.

"I just guess they did. If a horse was felled, a brother knight would ride up and say, 'Hop on, Sir Jack Galahad, there's lots of room for you.'"

Jack got to his feet. "Especially a brother knight who was a *brother*, I guess."

"For certain sure," said Tom as they climbed the bank.

Taking turns at lead position, they rode home, leaving on the riverbank a colored stick that had been Jack's war-horse, the mighty Brigadier.

In bed that night, Jack said dreamily, "Maybe one day we'll both be soldiers, Tom. And then our horses will not be toys."

Tom did not reply.

"Tom, did you hear me?"

"I heard. There would have to be a war, for us to be soldiers."

"Don't you want to be a soldier—astride a great war-horse, with a sword at your side?"

"A wooden horse is good enough for me."

"It won't be, if the real thing comes, an' there's rumors all 'round that it's comin'. Maybe not right away, but someday sure enough. And I hope it doesn't come 'n' go 'fore we're old enough."

"Old enough to go, you mean?"

"Well, o' course. You want to *miss* it?"

"You aren't even sure there'll be one."

"Oh, yes I am. Daddy says we won't put up forever with meddlin' Yankees tryin' to take away what's rightfully ours. There's no way 'round it, we'll have to fight to keep what belongs to us."

"Like Roger and Tulitha?"

"Not just them. All the rest. And our way of life. We have to protect that. Our honor's at stake. That's what Daddy says."

Tom raised up to lean on one elbow and stare across at his brother.

"Jack?"

"That's me."

"Remember the day you fell in the river and

Aaron saved you from drowning?"

"I recollect fallin' in, right enough. But Aaron didn't save my life. No way did he do that."

Tom blinked. "Jack! You were practically over the falls when he reached you."

"No such a thing. I was all set to swim ashore when he grabbed me. Playin' at bein' a hero, I s'pose."

"He wasn't playing at anything. He saved your life. You can't have forgot that!"

"You know, Brother Tom, you got a real bad bump in your memory place. You oughta have it seen to. G'night. I'm asleep." He gave a loud fake snore and pulled the pillow over his head.

Tom lay there, biting his lip, remembering that day years ago when Aaron had taken them to the river to fish.

He guessed they'd been about four years old. Jack, already far more daring physically than Tom, had suddenly tossed his pole aside and started across the stream, leaping from stone to stone.

Aaron had jumped up, shouting, "Jack! Y'all come on back here this minute! You hear me?"

As he turned to laugh at the two fraidycats, Jack slipped, fell into the rapid waters, and was carried off, screaming in terror.

Racing partway down the bank, Aaron dove into the river and caught Jack's arm just short of the ledge over which the waters were plunging.

They'd never told anyone about the episode, fearing Aaron would be sent from them for not being a proper watchdog. In those days, Jack had loved Aaron almost as much as Tom did.

No more, Tom thought, his lids drooping. Jack doesn't love or miss Aaron at all. And he and I—

we're changing, too. I don't want us to change. I don't think Jack wants it either. But it's happening.

The following year, on their birthday, the boys got horses from their father. Real live prancy high-spirited mounts. They named them Brigadier and Pompety, of course.

Roger carried Tom's wooden Pompety up to the vast attic, where it gathered dust in a dim corner, forgotten.

Now they could *really* play at tourney, at battle, at Crusades, at steeplechasing. They could race each other, or ride peacefully side by side, down the mile-long elm-lined lane.

They were still always together but didn't speak in the old way, as if each knew what the other was thinking. It was as if now they were afraid to know each other's thoughts.

They never spoke of Aaron. Jack because he scarcely recalled the days when Aaron had been a central part of their lives. Tom because it was what he couldn't forget.

In deference to what he considered some fraidycat silliness on Tom's part, Jack no longer dreamed aloud about how they'd grow up to be soldiers riding great war-horses into battle, beheading Yankees with their swords, crushing Yankees beneath their hooves.

He spoke no more of the glory of war. But war, above everything else, was what Jack wished for.

CHAPTER FOUR

W AR WAS WHAT HE GOT.

Ten years later, the North and South went to war against each other.

"It's like two brothers," said Mrs. Rigby, weeping. "Two bitter brothers, *hating* each other."

But on the plantations, in the towns of the South, there was jubilance.

"Oh, we'll show them," Jack shouted, pounding Tom on the back. "We'll rout and run those

Yankees off in a month's time!"

He raced to enlist, lest the war end before he got to it.

He strutted in his uniform of gray and red, peacocking up and down the veranda, flourishing his tasseled sword, stamping his boots with their silver spurs.

"Tom, Tom!" he said. "Sign up! Sign up! We'll ride into battle side by side, the way we dreamed of when we were boys!"

When Tom did not reply, Jack shook his arm. "Tom! Why do you delay?"

Tom sighed and said, "I leave today."

"To enlist! Make haste!"

"To enlist, yes. But I'll not be riding side by side with you, Jack. I ride north to enlist in the Union army."

A terrible silence followed Tom's words.

His mother's pain, his father's rage made him

sad, but most wounding of all was the look in his brother's eyes.

Traitor! that look said. Betrayer! Judas!

Giving Tom one last chance at redemption, Jack said, "You must be funnin', in a horrid horrible way! You don't mean what you say. You *can't* mean it."

"I do. I mean it."

Jack looked Tom up and down, as if assessing a stranger, then said slowly, "You are no longer my brother."

"You're wrong. We will always be brothers."

Jack turned on his heel and walked off, silver spurs jingling.

Late that afternoon, Tom rode alone on his roan horse, the second Pompety, down the mile-long elm-lined lane.

He did not want to ride into battle.

But if he must, it could never be to defend his

father's right to own people. To force them to sing in the baking fields from sunup to sundown. To put them in his pocket, selling them, like crockery, whenever he pleased.

Tom wanted his brother to understand how he felt.

"I understand what *you're* feelin'," he said aloud, as if Jack were at his side. "I think you're wrong, but I understand. *Why* can't you do the same for me?"

Pompety's ears flicked, as they always did at the sound of Tom's voice. They rode on. Sometimes Tom turned in the saddle, hoping for a wave from the veranda, a sign from Jack that they were brothers still. But the house was quiet as if empty, though he knew it was filled to brimming with his mother's anguish, his father's furious incomprehension.

With Jack's changeless enmity.

★ ★ ★

The armies of the South did not rout the armies of the North, nor run them off in a month's time. The dark tide of triumphs splashed from side to side for four halting years.

On an evening in August 1862, Lieutenant Tom Rigby, twenty-one years old this day, rode through a storm toward the encampment he called home.

Slumped in the saddle, almost sleeping, Tom jerked upright when his horse stumbled.

"Tired, are you?" he said, leaning to pat the drooping neck. "And hungry, too, I know. So am I hungry, and tired, and I haven't washed for days."

He'd been keeping his eyes down, to avoid the nightmare around him, but now a figure at the roadside grabbed his attention. A soldier in a bloodied rebel uniform sat, arms around his knees, quietly crying.

Dismounting, Tom approached the huddled figure.

"Jack?" he said. "Is it you, Jack?"

The soldier looked up and gasped for air. He was not, of course, Jack Rigby.

But this soldier was about Jack's age—and Tom's—and wounded, and weeping.

"Come along," said Tom. "You can ride back to camp with me. We'll get you to a hospital."

"A Union hospital?" the Reb stuttered.

"It'll be all right," Tom said. Most doctors and nurses were there to help, weren't they?

He said, "You'll be inside, at any rate. Out of the rain. And get something to eat."

"Your horse?" the Reb said weakly. "Can he manage?"

"He'll go just as well with . . . two—" Tom

caught his breath in remembrance of a weeping brother and a horse without a head on an afternoon long, long ago.

He hoisted his charge aboard, mounted behind him, and gently touched Pompety's flank. They rode through the rain for several miles before sighting camp.

The soldier spoke once. "You're trembling, Lieutenant."

"I know," said Tom. "From fatigue. From being drenched clear through. From the sound of cannon fire."

From remembering when Jack and I were two little boys, each with a wooden horse.

He did not speak aloud. Just plodded with his burden through the horror of this brothers' war.

STORYTELLER'S NOTE

MY MOTHER AND AUNT, twins, were born in the late nine-teenth century. Their father and uncles fought in the Union army and came home with stories and songs. For some reason, they sang this particular ballad so often that all these decades later I remember it word for word.

It gave me the idea for the book, and I like the continuity this implies.

—Mary Stolz

A Civil War Ballad

Once two little boys
had two little toys.
Each was a wooden horse.
Gaily they'd play
each summer's day,
"soldier boy," of course.

One little chap
had a mishap,
broke off his horse's head.
Wept for his toy,
then cried with joy
when his young comrade said:

"Did you think I would
leave you crying,
when there's room on my horse for two?
Hop on, dear Jack,
and don't be sighing.
He'll go just as well with two.

"Maybe someday we'll both be soldiers,
and our horses will not be toys.
And it may be that we'll remember
when we were two little boys."

Long years have passed—
war came at last.
Bravely they marched away.
Cannons roared loud,
and mid the mad crowd
wounded and dying
Jack lay.

Loud rings a cry!
A horse dashes by
from out of the ranks of Blue.
Gallops away
to where Jack lay,
And a voice rings clear and true.

"Did you think I would
leave you dying,
when there's room on my horse for two?
Jump up, dear Jack,
and don't be sighing,
He'll go just as well with two.

"Did you say, Jack, I'm all a-tremble?
Well, it may be the battle's noise.
Or it may be that I remember
when we were two little boys."